SUPERCHIMP

Giles Paley-Phillips

Illustrated by Karl Newson

Way down in the jungle...

...swinging through the trees,

is a **mighty superhero**
whose favourite food is fleas.

When animals are in trouble
and they give a little **yelp,**

from out of nowhere, Superchimp
appears to lend his help.

He's **FASTER** than a cheetah

and he's **STRONGER** than a bear.

He can *fly* just like an eagle

and he's got **red underwear!**

Everyone loves Superchimp
because he's strong and brave,

he's got a groovy chimpmobile

and a snazzy secret cave.

When baby Parrot flies too high
and gets stuck in a tree...

...her cries are heard by Superchimp
who helps to set her free.

When Lion has a splinter
and Hippo's stuck in muck,

Superchimp's on hand to help,
they just can't believe their luck.

"Superchimp's our hero!"

the animals all rejoice,

but far off in the distance,
they hear a booming voice.

"It's getting rather late young man, I think it's time for bed!"

In the moonlight, Mum appears
and Superchimp goes red.

Mum gives him a cuddle,
she can see he's gone quite shy.

"You can save your friends tomorrow,
for now let's say goodbye."

Being a hero is dangerous,

but it can be really fun.

Just don't ever stay out too late
because it might upset your mum!

Next Steps

Show the children the cover again. Could they have guessed what the story was about just by looking at the cover? Did any of the children think it would be a story about helping others?

Superchimp has many superpowers. Ask the children if they could have one superpower what would it be and why?

Superchimp helped lots of animals in the story. Can the children remember which animals he helped? How did he help them?

Does Superchimp enjoy helping others? Ask the children if they've ever helped someone or if someone else has helped them. How did it make them feel? Why is it important to help others?

Superchimp's favourite food is fleas! Ask the children if they'd ever eat fleas. Discuss with them what their favourite food is.

Near the end of the story, Superchimp hears a booming sound. Ask the children what they thought it might have been. You could discuss what noises you might hear in the jungle. Explain to the children that even superheroes feel frightened sometimes.

Did any of the children know what was going to happen to Superchimp at the end? Ask the children what they think Superchimp should do next time he goes out on a rescue mission.